Groundwood Books / House of Anansi Press
groundwoodbooks.com

We acknowledge for their financial support of our
publishing program the Canada Council for the Arts, the
Ontario Arts Council and the Government of Canada.

Library and Archives Canada Cataloguing in Publication
Vo, Nancy, author, illustrator
The outlaw / [written and illustrated by] Nancy Vo.
Issued in print and electronic formats.
ISBN 978-1-77306-016-3 (hardcover).—
ISBN 978-1-77306-017-0 (PDF)
I. Title.
PS8643.O2O98 2018   jC813'.6   C2017-905249-7
C2017-905250-0

Design by Michael Solomon
Printed and bound in Malaysia

Canada Council   Conseil des Arts
for the Arts   du Canada

ONTARIO ARTS COUNCIL
CONSEIL DES ARTS DE L'ONTARIO
an Ontario government agency
un organisme du gouvernement de l'Ontario

With the participation of the Government of Canada
Avec la participation du gouvernement du Canada   Canadä

For Mom and Dad

The illustrations were
done in ink, watercolor and
newsprint transfer on Rising
Stonehenge, using newspaper
clippings and fabric patterns from
the 1850s and 1860s. The title
was produced with wood type on
letterpress by Black Stone Press.
The text is set in Clarendon,
commonly found on "wanted"
posters.

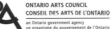

THE OUTLAW

NANCY VO

Groundwood Books   House of Anansi Press   Toronto   Berkeley

Once there was an outlaw.

Everyone knew of him by his trail of misdeeds.

Passengers worried, "Will the Outlaw plunder this train?"

Shopkeepers closed early. "Just in case."

CONDITION POWDERS
FOR HORSES

Pattern 21.b.

FOR MEDICINAL USE
PURE OLD
Rye Whisk

Children were warned, "Be good or else
the Outlaw will get you!"

Then, one day, the Outlaw stopped
coming into town entirely.
Everyone was relieved.
Everyone believed that he was as
good as gone.

Many seasons passed, until one hot windless
day, a stranger rode into town.

The town was a shadow of itself and in need of repair. Deftly, decisively, the stranger went to work.
First he built a water trough in front of the inn where he was staying.

Then he mended the roof of the old clapboard schoolhouse.

He was working on the train platform
when someone recognized him.

"You. You are the Outlaw!"

The stranger did not deny this.
One man kicked up dirt at him.
Another spat at his feet.
The Outlaw did nothing at all.

The boy stepped in front of the Outlaw.
"Leave him alone! He's trying."

Some saw the boy's point.

Some scowled and remained
unconvinced.

But convinced or not, eventually
the crowd departed.

So the Outlaw continued
to make amends.

And maybe that was what
mattered in the end.